The Pirate Queen

Story by Marianne Macdonald
Pictures by Jan Smith

BARRON'S

First edition for the United States published 1992
by Barron's Educational Series, Inc.

First published in Great Britain in 1991 by Orchard Books
96 Leonard Street, London EC2A 4RH.

All inquiries should be addressed to:
Barron's Educational Series, Inc.
250 Wireless Boulevard
Hauppauge, New York 11788

Library of Congress Catalog Card No. 92-4121

International Standard Book No. 0-8120-6288-4 (hardcover)
International Standard Book No. 0-8120-4952-7 (paperback)

Library of Congress Cataloging-in-Publication Data

Macdonald, Marianne.
    The Pirate Queen / story by Marianne Macdonald : pictures by Jan
Smith. — 1st ed. for the U.S.
        p.   cm.
    "First published in Great Britain 1991 by Orchard Books"—T.p.
verso.
    Summary: A young girl imagines that she is Queen of all the
Pirates and turns her ordinary surroundings into exotic settings for
her adventures.
    ISBN 0-8120-6288-4. — ISBN 0-8120-4952-7 (pbk.)
    [1. Pirates—Fiction. 2. Imagination—Fiction. 3. Play—
Fiction.] I. Smith, Jan, ill. II. Title.
PZ7.M14854P1   1992
[E]—dc20   92-4121
                                                                   CIP
                                                                   AC

Printed in Belgium

2345   987654321

Maggie was a pirate.

She had a big black pirate ship. It was called
The Pirate Queen. It had big black sails, and the
skull-and-crossbones flag flew from the top of
the highest mast.

The crew were all desperate pirates, with knives between their teeth. But they all did what she told them, because *she* was Captain Maggie, the Queen of all the Pirates.

One morning, she put on her pirate hat and took her pirate sword, and she went downstairs. And she said to her mother. "Do you have a roasted ox? Because I am going on a voyage to look for treasure, and I am VERY HUNGRY."

Her mother said, "I don't have an ox all roasted just now, but you could have cornflakes and orange juice and toast and strawberry jam instead."

And she did.

Then she went and climbed aboard *The Pirate Queen*. And she told the pirates to raise the anchor and sail away in search of treasure.

And they did.

They sailed and they sailed until they came
to an island, and there on the island was a table
with a great big treasure chest. Maggie said to
the pirates, "Stop the ship!"

And they did.

Inside the treasure chest there were gold and silver and jewels. So she put on some golden earrings and a golden necklace and golden bracelets. And then they sailed away.

They sailed and they sailed until they came to the pirates' kitchen, where there was a bag full of magic paints and pencils.

Maggie said, "We'll give ourselves disguises now, and when we fight people they won't know who we are."

And they did.

And then they sailed away.

They sailed and they sailed until they came
to a country where there was a castle built of
wood. Maggie said to the pirates,
    "Stop the ship!"

She looked inside the castle, and there were some things: a chariot and some swords and daggers, all covered with jewels – diamonds and rubies and pearls.

And she said to the pirates, "Carry those things outside and pull the jewels off them and take them away."

So they did.

And then they sailed away.

They sailed and they sailed out to the open sea, and there they saw the treasure fleet. The Admiral had disguised his ships so that the pirates wouldn't see them. But when Maggie looked through her telescope, she recognized them at once.

And she said to her pirate crew, "Raise all our sails so that we go as fast as fast! There is the treasure fleet, and that one is the Admiral's galleon, full of gold. We will ram it, and jump on board, and fight the crew until they give us all the treasure."

So they did.

The Pirate Queen sailed close to the Admiral's galleon, and bumped into it hard, and the pirates all jumped on board, waving their swords. But the galleon capsized, and all its treasure fell into the sea, and Maggie was wounded on her knee.

So she told the pirates to sail home again, and she went into the kitchen and said to her mother, "Are you the ship's doctor? Because now I am wounded."

Her mother said, "I am not the ship's doctor. But I am the Great Ma. And I can cure your wound by magic. But if I do, you will be IN MY POWER."

And Maggie said, "Yes, please."
And the Great Ma washed her knee with cool water, and put on some magic ointment and a magic bandage.

Then the Great Ma took her magic wand and waved it and said,

Dibble-dabble, double-bubble,
Bibble-babble, pirate-trouble,
By flits and flutes and cauliflower,
NOW YOU ARE IN MY POWER!

"Now you will sail back and pick up that trash can and put all the trash back inside."

So they sailed back to the Admiral's galleon, and they pulled the ship upright and put back the treasure. And then they sailed home.

And the Great Ma waved her magic wand and said,

Dibble-dabble, double-bubble,
Bibble-babble, pirate-trouble,
By flits and flutes and cauliflower,
YOU ARE IN MY POWER!

"Now you will go into the backyard and put all those things back in the shed."

So Maggie told her pirates to put everything away, and they did. And then they sailed home.

(But they kept the jewels, because the Great Ma didn't say anything about those.)

And the Great Ma took her magic wand and said,

> Dibble-dabble, double-bubble,
> Bibble-babble, pirate-trouble,
> By flits and flutes and cauliflower,
> NOW YOU ARE IN MY POWER!

Now you will go up to my bedroom and take my jewelery off and put it away – neatly, now!"